Bantam Books in the Choose Your Own Adventure® Series
Ask your bookseller for the books you have missed.

Choose Your Own Adventure® Books for younger readers

SECRET OF THE PYRAMIDS

BY RICHARD BRIGHTFIELD

An Edward Packard Book

ILLUSTRATED BY ANTHONY KRAMER

BANTAM BOOKS
TORONTO · NEW YORK · LONDON · SYDNEY

RL4, IL Age 10 and Up

SECRET OF THE PYRAMIDS
A Bantam Book / April 1983

Original Conception of Edward Packard

ISBN 0-553-23295-9

Published simultaneously in the United States and Canada

---

*Bantam Books are published by Bantam Books, Inc. Its trade-
mark, consisting of the words "Bantam Books" and the por-
trayal of a rooster, is Registered in U.S. Patent and Trademark
Office and in other countries. Marca Registrada. Bantam
Books, Inc., 666 Fifth Avenue, New York, New York 10103.*

PRINTED IN THE UNITED STATES OF AMERICA

O   0 9 8 7 6 5 4 3 2 1

To Glory and Savitri

WARNING!!!!

Do not read this book straight through from beginning to end! These pages contain many different adventures you can have in the land of the Pyramids. From time to time as you read along, you will be asked to make a choice. Your choice may lead to success or disaster.

The adventures you take are a result of your choices. *You* are responsible because *you* choose. After you make each choice, follow the instructions to see what happens to you next.

Think carefully before you make a move. Any choice might be your last . . . or it *may* lead you to the secret of the Pyramids.

Good luck!

You are relaxing one afternoon after school when you get a phone call from your uncle Bruce, a brilliant scientist and world traveler.

"I'm just in from Egypt," he says. "I have to get some new equipment to continue my investigations of the Pyramids. How would you like to go back with me for a few weeks?"

You have always envied Bruce—dashing off to exotic places in the Middle East and the Orient, sometimes vanishing for months at a time. It doesn't take you long to make up your mind to go.

Go on to page 2.

The next few days are a blur of preparations. Before you know it, you and Bruce are on a TWA jet heading for Rome on the first leg of the trip to Cairo.

On the plane, your uncle explains his plan to place special instruments in a chamber under the center of the largest pyramid at Giza. He hopes to test the pyramid's effect on the paths of cosmic rays—rays made up of high-speed particles from space that usually penetrate deep into the ground.

"If my theory is correct," he says, "these rays could be concentrated by the pyramid to produce an unlimited amount of energy."

While Bruce is talking, you notice that a man nearby is straining to hear him. No doubt he's just curious. He is strange-looking, though!

In Rome you change to an Egyptair jet. You are startled to notice the same man from the other jet aboard your Cairo-bound plane.

"I will have lots of red tape to take care of at the airport when we land," says Bruce. "Why don't you just breeze through customs and take a cab to the Star and Crescent Hotel, where we're staying? My assistant, Andrea, will be waiting there for you. She can get you settled in our room while my equipment is unloaded from the plane."

As soon as you land, Bruce is off to the baggage area, leaving you alone in a foreign land. As if that isn't enough, the stranger from the plane appears and hands you a small, folded piece of paper, then dashes toward the taxi stand outside the terminal.

Quickly you unfold the note. Scrawled in red ink are the words "Beware the Sphinx."

You have heard about the statue of the Sphinx next to the Pyramids. But why should you beware of it? The thought occurs to you that "sphinx" could be a code word and not refer to the actual Sphinx at all. Maybe the note is a meaningless hoax. On the other hand, it could spell danger for you and Bruce.

You remember the time you felt an urge to get off a bus in your hometown—just before it was hit by a truck. Now you have a hunch that you should follow this man.

If you try to follow him, turn to page 13.

If you decide that it is wiser to go to your hotel, go on to page 4.

There's no telling what kind of trouble you might get into if you just run off after this guy without really knowing where you are going.

You toss your bag into the back of a cab.

"Star and Crescent Hotel," you tell the driver.

When you arrive, Andrea is waiting for you in the lobby. She helps you check in.

The bellboy insists on carrying your bag, even though you are traveling light. As you leave the elevator and head for your room, you could swear that the door, which was slightly ajar, closed as you approached. Maybe it was the wind, but the air seems very still. And after that warning note at the airport, you don't want to take any chances.

"Wait," you say. "I don't want this room. I don't like the location."

The bellboy looks confused, and Andrea seems shocked. You haven't had a chance to tell her about the note.

"I'll explain later," you tell Andrea. "Right now I'm going to go back down to the lobby and ask for a different room."

But at the check-in desk, the clerk will not listen to you. What will you do?

If you threaten to go to another hotel unless the clerk changes your room, turn to page 32.

If you decide you're imagining things and let the clerk talk you into taking your original room, turn to page 36.

"They must have hit us with a grenade," Mohammed says. "It's a good thing this limo is armor-plated."

Mohammed has been on the two-way police radio from the moment you jumped into the car. Now information comes back that the police are surrounding the area.

"They won't catch anyone," says Mohammed. "These terrorists are professionals. They will disappear back into the old quarter of the city in a matter of minutes."

Two police jeeps arrive almost immediately. Policemen begin to fan out around the area. You and Mohammed transfer to one of the jeeps, and it speeds off to Inspector Ahmed's villa, its siren wailing.

Turn to page 31.

Bruce finally agrees to let you stay awhile longer. "But we'll have to be very careful," he warns.

Neither of you is in the mood to go back to sleep. You leave a note under Andrea's door and go down to the lobby. Even though it is only the earliest dawn, the back streets of Cairo are bustling with activity. At one of the broader intersections, you find a cab and direct the driver to take you to Giza.

When you arrive, an Egyptian friend of your uncle is already there: Mr. Hassan, the Egyptian Director of Antiquities. It was Hassan who first persuaded your uncle to come to Egypt many years ago.

The three of you look down into the deep pit that contains the entrance to the tunnel under the pyramid. Nearby the Sphinx sits in its ageless pose.

"We had a slight problem finishing the tunnel," says Hassan. "The workmen claimed that the Sphinx itself spoke to them, saying 'Beware the Sphinx.' "

Turn to page 62.

8

The driver steps out.

"This is Mohammed," says the inspector, introducing his bodyguard. "Enjoy your sight-seeing."

Mohammed drives you out to the famous Pyramids at Giza. A group of tourists is gathering at the foot of the largest one.

"Why don't we join this group?" suggests Mohammed. "It is the safest way, and you will find it informative."

You have never liked official tours of any sort—you are too independent—but you see the logic of Mohammed's suggestion. As the group starts into the pyramid, you and Mohammed fall in behind. You enter a low, narrow passageway which leads to a large gallery with a high ceiling. The guide begins a long, dull lecture.

"Do we have to follow this tour?" you ask Mohammed.

"If I may presume to suggest an alternative," says Mohammed, "I myself was once employed as a guide in this very pyramid. If you would like me to show you some of the lesser passageways, I would be glad to guide you."

If you accept Mohammed's invitation, turn to page 34.

If the narrow passageways are making you feel closed in, turn to page 74.

Just as you get to the wall, a panel opens and reveals a lighted niche. Inside is a very elaborate and jeweled costume—a ceremonial costume of ancient Egypt. The humming grows even louder now. You feel compelled to exchange your clothes for the long robe, the headdress, and the sandals in front of you. You put them on. You want to stop yourself, but you can't.

Turn to page 63.

Bruce seemingly agrees to cooperate, and Ptah is delighted. Bruce is sent under guard to work in the laboratory located in a vast complex under the pyramid.

A few days later, Bruce manages to talk to you without the guards overhearing.

"The Russian scientists were also kidnapped," whispers Bruce. "Fortunately I can speak a little Russian. We're trying to come up with a way to escape."

Three weeks later, the ray gun is ready for its first formal test. You, Bruce, and the Russians—as well as Ptah and his top henchmen—mount a large ceremonial stand in front of the pyramid. As Ptah watches the barrel of the ray gun emerge from the top of the pyramid, Bruce slips something into your hand.

"Put these plugs in your ears when I give you the signal," Bruce whispers.

Technicians inside the pyramid throw the switches to activate the ray gun. A low whirring sound fills the air. It rises in pitch as it gets louder—louder and louder, and higher and higher. Soon it begins to hurt your ears. Your arms and legs become numb, and your vision starts to blur.

Turn to page 75.

"Inspector . . . Inspector Ahmed!" sputters the clerk.

"What is the trouble here?" asks the inspector.

"My uncle has been kidnapped from the hotel," you say.

"Is your uncle Professor Hockney?" asks the inspector.

"How did you know?"

"I have been watching this hotel since he arrived. I was afraid something like this might happen."

"I think I saw the kidnappers in a truck behind the hotel," you report anxiously.

You and the inspector run to the back entrance of the hotel, but the truck is gone.

Turn to page 44.

The strange man is already in a cab when you reach the stand in front of the terminal. You manage to jump into the next cab in line.

"Do you speak English?" you ask.

"I speak much English, *meestehr.*"

"Good, then follow that cab," you tell him.

Your cab weaves in and out of the heavy traffic, with its horn blaring constantly. Your driver just barely misses one car after another. However, he does manage to keep less than a block behind the other car.

The fast-moving traffic slows to a snail's pace once you get into an older section of the city. The cab you are following stops, and the strange man gets out. You hand your driver a couple of American bills, hoping they cover your fare. Fortunately, the driver seems more than pleased as you leave the cab.

You can barely see through the thick crowd, but you do catch a glimpse of the man you are following. He is entering what looks like a café. You push your way over to the entrance.

Turn to page 37.

14

You tell Ahmed that you would rather go back to the hotel, try to find Andrea, and get her opinion before you do anything.

You return to the hotel in a cab and check Andrea's room. No sign of her. You leave the hotel not quite knowing what to do.

At the corner a native woman, with a dark veil covering her head and face, except for the eyes, beckons from a doorway. You are surprised to see that her eyes are pale gray. You are even *more* surprised when you hear her voice. The woman is Andrea in disguise!

"Follow me quickly," she says.

You have to run to keep up with her. She leads you through a labyrinth of teeming alleyways. Finally you reach a stone building with a heavy, carved door.

Turn to page 106.

There may be dangers involved, but you can't let your uncle down. You tell the inspector you will go with him on the raid.

"We will leave at dawn tomorrow," says Ahmed. "It is not advisable for you to go back to your hotel. My personal bodyguard will escort you today, and tonight he will bring you to my home, where you will spend the night. Perhaps you would like to tour the Pyramids today."

"It might keep my mind off Bruce until tomorrow," you say.

"Then let's step outside," Ahmed says.

As you do, a long, black Mercedes limousine pulls up.

"This car is bulletproof, among other things," says Ahmed. "You will find it quite comfortable—and safe."

Turn to page 8.

You slide down the drainpipe to the balcony below, and then begin to lower yourself to the street. You try not to look down. Carefully you reach around with your foot for whatever footholds you can find sticking out from the building. It is easier than you had expected.

Finally you make it down to the street. You can still see the truck. It's only a block away, stuck in traffic. You push your way through the crowded street as fast as you can to catch up to it.

Out of breath, you reach the back of the truck. You jump on and struggle with the doors. They fly open suddenly, and you fall back onto the street, banging your knee. Hopping painfully on one leg, you get up and pull yourself into the truck.

Turn to page 53.

A screen slowly appears in one of the walls, and what looks like a movie about ancient Egypt begins. You see a pyramid being built. Workers scurry about with ropes and long poles. But they do not carry the huge blocks of stone. The stones float through the air by themselves!

A few of the workers
carry devices which project a
beam of light onto the blocks
and cause them to rise in the air. Other workers
toss ropes over the enormous floating blocks and
lead them along, while the workers with the poles
push the blocks gently into place. Amazing!

Turn to page 50.

Another guard appears at the door of the room.

"Ahmed won't be coming back," he says. "All of us left at the villa are members of the Assassins. We have infiltrated Ahmed's organization."

Two other members of the Assassins enter the room, guns drawn. They lead you down to a dungeon in the basement of the villa and chain you to an iron ring set in the stone wall.

You realize that you're going to be a "guest" of the Assassins for a very long time.

The End

"That looks as if it might be a kind of monorail," says Bruce. "See, that big plastic bubble travels on the rail out through a circular tunnel on the far side. I've suspected for a long time that something like this might exist. It confirms a theory of mine that ancient Egyptian culture was given a big boost by a more advanced one."

The door of the bubble is open, and Bruce jumps inside. His hand sweeps over the complex control panel.

"I think I see how this thing works," says Bruce. "Let's give it a try. Of course, we don't know what dangers lie ahead. This time," Bruce says to you, "you definitely should stay behind to go for help—just in case we don't get back."

If you insist on going along, turn to page 97.

If you stay behind, turn to page 49.

It is suddenly very quiet in the next room.

"Bruce, are you all right?" you call through the door. There is no answer. You throw open the door. Bruce is gone!

The room is a mess. Sheets trail across the floor as if a struggle had taken place. In several places there are drops of blood. The screen covering the window has been pushed in. There are more spots of blood on the windowsill and on the small ledge outside. You look down. There is a four-story drop to the street.

You rush back into your room and throw on some clothes. Then back to the window. It is a bit lighter now. Dawn is just breaking. On the street you see two men, loading a large basket into the back of an old panel truck. From this height—and in the still-dim light—you can't be sure, but something tells you that one of them is the stranger who gave you the note. You also have a strong suspicion that your uncle is in the basket. How did they get him down to the street?

The ledge outside the window extends only a short distance on either side. There are no other windows nearby. But there are several small balconies on the second and third floors. There is also a drainpipe on one side of the ledge. Maybe you could slide down the drainpipe to the nearest balcony and then climb down to the street.

You're in a panic. What should you do?

If you decide to risk climbing down the side of the building, turn to page 17.

If you decide to get the police, turn to page 59.

One by one you, Bruce, and Hassan slide down the rope into the chamber below. It is a large room. In the center are huge chunks of rock and other debris that must have fallen from the ceiling. At one end of the room is a door leading to another chamber.

As you approach the door it opens automatically. This startles all of you for a moment. Carefully you peer inside. You are hardly prepared for what you see.

The room is illuminated with some kind of strange light. The walls and ceiling are made of a plastic material with a honeycomb pattern, and they seem to glow with an inner luminescence. In the center, perched on a glistening metal rail, is some kind of futuristic device.

Turn to page 21.

It is very late when you get back to the hotel. You are weary from the plane trip and the experiences of the day. You fall asleep instantly. Bruce is in the adjoining room.

At dawn, something startles you awake. You hear sounds of a struggle in Bruce's room. Quick as a cat, you spring out of bed and run to the door.

Turn to page 23.

The throne room is a large circular hall surrounded by ornate columns, decorated in the style of ancient Egypt.

"Ah, my friends. Sit over here by the fountain," says a short man wearing a large turban overloaded with jewels and multicolored feathers. "I'm so glad that you accepted my invitation to visit. I see that you two appear to have bumped your heads together. Most unfortunate. I'll see to it that my infirmary looks after your injuries."

Turn to page 68.

"If it will help me rescue Bruce, I'll join," you say.

"Then step into the triangle on the ground in front of you," says the speaker.

You look down. Strange—the triangle has the same design as the coin you tossed down the shaft, only much larger. As you step forward, a strong energy floods through you, and an intense light surrounds your body. You close your eyes but the light's brightness does not diminish.

Suddenly you are caught up in a whirlwind and shot straight up through the pyramid. You look down and see the pyramid receding below you. The top of the pyramid has become a huge, glistening eye, shooting rays of light in all directions. Below it are bands of glowing color. As you concentrate on the eye, your body seems to dissolve. You become the eye—all-seeing, all-knowing. Your mind expands to encompass the universe, to fill infinite space. All the mysteries of existence are now understandable.

Your mind and body return to earth. Suddenly you *know* where Bruce is being held. With your new powers you contact him telepathically. Later the police are amazed when you are able to lead them directly to the hideout of the Assassins— where Bruce has been imprisoned—in one of the old quarters of Cairo.

From now on, you will find a whole new life of joy and dangers.

The End

Quickly you wrap the pillow around the snake, dash to the closet, hurl the snake and pillow inside, and slam the closet door shut.

You stand for a full minute with your back against the door. Your heart is still pounding. You feel weak in the knees as you realize what you've just done.

You wake your uncle and tell him about the snake.

"First that warning note—and now this attack!" exclaims Bruce. "It seems that someone is out to stop our little expedition by any means."

"But why?" you ask.

"I may be closer than I thought to unlocking the secret of unlimited energy. At least someone out there seems to think so. We'd better get you back to the States before something worse happens."

If you agree to go home, turn to page 89.

If you plead with Bruce to let you stay, turn to page 7.

"Let's get to the car."

"There's an exit to our right that doesn't seem to be covered," says Mohammed. "I will count to five. Then we will get up from the table and move as quickly as we can out that door. Don't run unless they start shooting, then keep low. Ready? One, two, three, four, five."

Your feet feel like lead, and even though you know you are moving as fast as you can, it feels like slow motion. Somehow you make it through the exit and into the car. You look back to see armed figures running in your direction. The car roars away from the curb. WHAM! Something smacks the car with terrific force.

Turn to page 5.

"I must compliment you on your escape," says Ahmed, when you arrive. "It was your cool-headedness that saved you."

"It was really Mohammed's quick thinking that did it," you reply.

"Now that you see what kind of dangers we face," says Ahmed, "I will understand if you change your mind about joining the raid tomorrow."

If you still want to go on the raid, turn to page 80.

If you've had enough of this terrorist business, and prefer to wait at the villa, turn to page 78.

Your threat of going to another hotel seems to do the trick. The clerk sighs and mutters something about tourists. Nevertheless, he directs the porter to carry your bag to a new room.

"What is this all about?" asks Andrea.

"I'm not sure myself, but a man at the airport handed me a warning note. If we are in danger, changing our room may throw our pursuer off, or at least show him we are on our guard."

"Well, I think this is a lot of nonsense," Andrea says.

Your new "suite" consists of two small rooms with a connecting door. The first room is windowless; the second has a small window covered by a screen of very elaborate grillwork. Andrea's room is on the other side of the hotel, not far from your original room.

Bruce arrives a short time later. You tell him about the warning note and explain why you've changed rooms.

"Splendid!" he exclaims. "You must always follow your hunches, especially when danger is involved. Now I suggest that we go out on the town for the evening. You don't want to miss the Sahara Club and its famous belly dancers."

Turn to page 26.

"I think we had better go down to my office," says Ahmed. "I want you to look through my photo file."

The inspector's office at headquarters is cluttered but organized in its own way. A row of file cabinets lines one side of the room. Ahmed pulls out a folder, opens it on one of the few bare sections of his long desk, and spreads out a collection of photographs for you to study.

Somehow you are not surprised to see the man from the plane in one of the photos. You tell Ahmed the whole story.

"The man you recognize is a member of the Assassins," says Ahmed. "This just confirms what I told you before. Through informers, I have discovered the secret desert headquarters of the Assassins. There is a strike force of paratroopers and a dozen helicopters waiting to attack. We must act as soon as possible."

"If you are going to raid the hideout of the kidnappers," you say, "I think I should go along."

"It is true that Professor Hockney *is* your uncle," says Ahmed. "However, this mission may prove to be very dangerous. I advise you not to go, but of course the decision is yours."

*If you decide to go along on the raid,
turn to page 16.*

*If you decide that it is too dangerous,
turn to page 14.*

"Anything would be better than this lecture," you say. "Those other passageways sound exciting."

You follow Mohammed into a narrow tunnel. At one point he stops and feels along the wall. One of the stones in the wall slides back, and a small, very low door opens.

"Quickly," says Mohammed, "we must get inside before anyone comes." Mohammed enters the long, horizontal shaft. The passageway is so low that you have to crawl on your hands and knees. You hear a click as the stone door behind you slides back into place. You hope Mohammed knows where he is going!

You and Mohammed crawl for quite a while. Finally you come to a large square chamber. The walls are white with blue and gold hieroglyphs painted in neat rows around the room. In the exact center of the floor is a round hole.

"That is what we call the Well of the Ancients," says Mohammed.

"You mean that you can draw water from down there?"

"There are many things other than water that can be drawn from a well—wisdom, perhaps," replies Mohammed. "This well is very deep. Here—drop this in the well and see if you can hear when it hits bottom."

Go on to the next page.

Mohammed hands you a small coin. It is triangular with an elaborate design in the center. A tiny, just barely visible hieroglyphic inscription runs around the edge. The coin shines as if made of gold.

You throw the coin in and put your ear close to the well. For a full minute you hear nothing. Then you hear a strange humming—a high musical note that vibrates both in the well and inside your head. You turn to look at Mohammed, but he seems to have disappeared.

Suddenly you feel as if you are losing your balance. You are falling into the well.

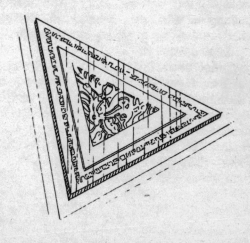

Turn to page 65.

Maybe jet lag and your imagination are getting the best of you.

"Never mind," you tell the desk clerk.

You go back up to the room and unpack your small suitcase. You make a careful search. There is no sign that an intruder has been there, and you feel relieved. Your room turns out to be a suite, with a bedroom, a sitting room, a small bathroom, and two tiny closets. The bedroom windows are covered with elaborately patterned grillwork. Andrea's room is on the same floor, down the hall.

Bruce finally arrives and you show him the note. For a moment he looks alarmed. Then he smiles. "Well, I suggest we forget about it for the moment and go out on the town," he says. "I know this great spot called the Sahara Club where we can get a delicious meal of shish kebab—and even watch some genuine Egyptian belly dancing."

When you arrive back at the hotel later, you are very tired. Andrea goes to her room, Bruce retires to the bedroom, and you quickly fall asleep on the couch in the sitting room.

Turn to page 42.

The rhythmic beat of Middle Eastern music hits your ears as you go inside. There is a heavy smell of incense. A belly dancer sways in the center of the dance floor. You find a table off in a dim corner. You can't see the man you followed, but your eyes are still adjusting to the darkness.

Turn to page 96.

"We've got to go down there now. My uncle may be in grave danger."

You and Ahmed start down the side of the dune toward the pyramids.

Suddenly a troop of desert warriors on camels appears from nowhere and comes charging toward you. Dark headcloths cover their faces except for their eyes. But instead of the old, long rifles you have seen them carrying in pictures, they all have modern submachine guns—and they are all pointed at you.

One of the warriors commands you to raise your hands and march toward the pyramids.

A door opens in the base of one of the smaller pyramids, and you and Ahmed are forced into the vault inside. The door snaps shut behind you. You realize that the "floor" you're standing on is a conveyor belt that is rapidly carrying you toward a wall of flame at the other end of the vault. You try frantically to run back to the door, but the belt is too fast. You are both swept into the thermal chamber—a chamber that so concentrates the energy of the sun that any object entering it is instantly vaporized.

The End

As you start to leave the platform, the approaching figure greets you.

"My name is Imhotep. I greet you from the past."

"For a while there I thought we were *in* the past," you say.

"No, I am not actually here at the moment, and you are not back in ancient Egypt. This is a recording—a three-dimensional hologram. My image is programmed to respond to individual personalities such as yours. Even though you may feel my arm as solid—here, I will touch your hand—it is only an illusion. It is too complex to explain, but your descendants will understand someday, just as *you* know that when you listen to a radio there are not little people in the box making the sounds."

"You are the most celebrated character in Egyptian history," says Hassan. "You were—or are—the greatest genius that ever lived."

"It is true that I gave your species a bit of help. I taught them the rudiments of architecture, farming, mathematics, engineering, and medicine. That was five thousand years ago. But I am not sure I was wise to do it. I will have to decide that when I find time to return. Your planet is in my study quadrant, but it is far out on the edge of the galaxy."

As he speaks, the image of Imhotep seems to blur a bit.

Turn to page 56.

You, Bruce, and Hassan climb down a ladder into the deep pit. At the bottom, a six-foot-square opening penetrates the side wall. A perfectly straight tunnel of the same dimensions goes into the rock—horizontal for a short way, then sloping sharply downward. The three of you enter it.

A hand rope along the wall keeps you from slipping. Your flashlight beams cut into the darkness ahead. Finally you come to a circular room about twelve feet in diameter, directly beneath the center of the pyramid.

"This is strange, *very* strange," says Hassan. "Yesterday this floor was completely smooth, almost polished. Now there is a pattern of cracks over here and part of the floor has sunk."

Suddenly there is a cracking noise.

"Get back to the tunnel!" shouts Bruce. "The floor is caving in."

Turn to page 70.

Toward early morning some inner instinct half-awakens you. You hear a faint rustling and the sound of a door softly clicking shut. You snap on the small table lamp. Only inches away from your face is an asp, one of the deadliest snakes in the world.

You've got seconds before it strikes.

If you grab your pillow and try to clamp it down on the snake, turn to page 29.

If you back off slowly and call your uncle for help, turn to page 88.

"I shouldn't have waited," you say, downcast. "I should have climbed down the wall of the hotel and tried to stop them before they got away."

"No," says the inspector, "you did the right thing. These men are fanatics. They probably would have shot you down."

"You know the men who did this?"

"They are members of an ancient terrorist group known as the Society of Assassins. They know that your uncle is working on a way to produce enormous amounts of energy. They would like to steal this secret and use it for their own evil plans."

"Did Bruce know they were after him?"

"He did, but he is always exposing himself to danger. A most peculiar man, your uncle, if you will pardon my saying so."

"Some people might feel that way," you say.

"In any event," says the inspector, "he is a brave man, too, and I have failed to protect him. I feel responsible for your uncle's disappearance. I will do everything in my power to find him."

"First," you say, "I think we should go upstairs and wake up Bruce's assistant, Andrea."

The two of you go to Andrea's room. Inspector Ahmed knocks on the door. No answer. The door is unlocked. You and Ahmed go in. No Andrea!

Turn to page 33.

You feel that you would like to get your feet on the ground, at least.

Ahmed flies low over the sand, looking for a stone outcropping that might give you protection from the storm. Below you the sand is being driven across the desert in little whirlwinds.

Ahmed shouts your approximate position into the radio, though it's doubtful anyone can hear over the noise of the storm. He grabs a piece of canvas from the back of the cockpit just as the two of you jump from the helicopter. Seconds later a powerful gust picks the helicopter up and sends it tumbling along the ground like a fragile toy.

Go on to page 46.

You dive to protect your face from the pebbles and sharp rock hurled through the air by the wind. You are temporarily blinded. Your lungs fill with choking dust.

"Up against this ridge," shouts Ahmed. "We must imitate camels in a storm. Kneel, head to the ground, away from the wind.

"Here," he shouts. "Help spread this cover over us. This sand will wear away our clothing in no time. Then it will start on our flesh."

The sun must be up, but it is now pitch dark. The roaring of the wind is still so loud that Ahmed must yell directly into your ear for you to hear what he is saying.

"We must shift our weight every few minutes to knock the sand off our backs—otherwise we'll be buried alive," he cries.

You are now choking almost to suffocation. Your arms and legs have lost their feeling.

Turn to page 85.

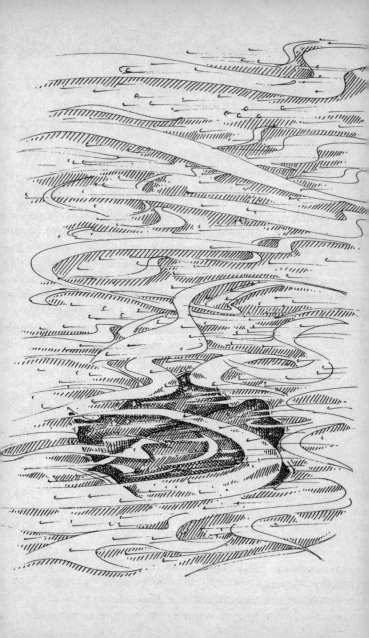

Your uncle and Hassan go off in the strange bubblecraft. Now that they are gone, you wish you had insisted on going with them. It is lonely waiting by yourself.

As you wait, you begin to hear some kind of humming. At first the sound is very low. Then it gets louder and louder. It seems to come from a specific spot on the wall. You walk toward it.

Turn to page 10.

"This looks like some kind of science-fiction movie," you say.

"I don't think it's science fiction," says Bruce. "I think we're seeing the real thing."

"Don't be ridiculous," says Hassan. "Every archaeologist knows that it took thousands of workers scores of years to build the Pyramids."

Bruce shakes his head. "Those blocks weigh two to three tons each. They were fitted together so carefully that not even the thinnest piece of paper can be slipped into the joints. Does anyone *really* know how they got those blocks there?"

The picture blurs. A kind of fog drifts over the screen and then clears away. The pyramid is completed. But what a pyramid! It appears to be early morning. The top third of the pyramid is sheathed in gold, polished to a mirror finish. The rest of the pyramid is painted in iridescent colors in horizontal stripes clear to the bottom.

The early sunlight strikes the top of the pyramid and throws a blinding shaft of light straight up into the sky.

You are so fascinated by this scene that it takes you several minutes to realize that the triangular viewscreen is gradually growing larger.

As you watch, the entire wall of the room becomes a viewscreen, and the other three walls vanish completely. The glowing floor remains, but you seem to be standing in ancient Egypt!

Go on to the next page.

A figure who appears to be a priest or high official seems to notice you from afar. He comes closer and beckons to the three of you.

"If we leave this platform, do you think we can get back?" you ask Bruce.

"I have no idea how the mechanism operates," Bruce replies. "I'm not even sure we're any safer if we stay where we are."

If you decide to stay where you are, turn to page 76.

If you decide to leave the platform, turn to page 39.

The truck jerks to a stop. The kidnappers must have heard the door open. They reach the back of the truck just as you are trying to open the basket. One of the men is a hulking brute; the other man is the one you saw on the plane and in the airport. They have you boxed in. No use calling for help. No one could hear you over the noise outside.

Turn to page 60.

Mohammed disappears in the direction of the phone. You sit, waiting—and wishing he would come back. One by one, the people at nearby tables finish their drinks and leave. You suddenly realize that you are alone in the café.

Then you become aware that there are shadowy figures, each with a submachine gun, standing behind the large pillars around the café. The guns open up at you all at once.

The End

There in the distance, before your eyes, a pyramid emerges out of the sand like the bow of an enormous submarine. Smaller pyramids rise to encircle it, their surfaces flashing in the sun with the brilliance of polished gold. Bolts of artificial lightning jump from the top of the large pyramid to the tops of the smaller ones, causing booming sounds to reverberate across the desert.

"This is incredible!" exclaims Ahmed. "I've never seen anything like it. I've heard stories of strange devices that can concentrate the sun's energy to almost unimaginable levels. I'm not sure, but I think that is what we are looking at."

"I'm sure this is what my uncle was experimenting with," you cry. "We've got to investigate. Bruce may be a captive down there."

"I don't like the looks of this at all," says Ahmed. "I think it would be better for us to slip away and try to get help."

If you convince Ahmed that it is important to investigate now, turn to page 38.

If you let Ahmed convince you to slip away, turn to page 58.

"I apologize for the brevity of our meeting," continues Imhotep. "I hope your civilization prospers. Someday you or your descendants will come across the vastness of space to visit *me*. You will be welcome. For now, farewell."

The image begins to fade and you find yourselves back inside the pyramid room. The outside door reopens, and the three of you return the way you came.

"I think we should keep this discovery a secret among the three of us," says Bruce.

"I quite agree," Hassan says. "The world is not yet ready for this knowledge."

You agree too.

The next day you watch as workmen fill in the tunnel. When you leave the site, you go past the Sphinx. Perhaps you only imagine that it says: "You will be welcome someday."

The End

58

"I think you are right," you say. "We might be walking into a trap."

You and Ahmed slip carefully down the tall dune.

"Let us head south for a few hours and then go west again," says Ahmed.

You both take the last sips of water from the canteen.

"We can last another four hours without water," adds Ahmed. "After that, dehydration will finish us."

After several hours of trudging across the sand, you barely have enough strength to keep moving. Your throat is so dry that you can't swallow. Bright spots dance before your eyes—a sign that you are dying of thirst.

Turn to page 99.

Climbing down the side of the building is too risky, you think. One slip, and . . . ! You wouldn't be much help to your uncle then.

You run down to the lobby and quickly explain the situation to the desk clerk.

"I told you that you should have kept the room you were assigned," says the clerk smugly. "But if you are in need of emergency assistance, I will do what I can."

He picks up the hotel phone and clicks for the operator. At that moment a policeman enters the hotel lobby. The surprised clerk hangs up the phone and looks at him openmouthed.

Turn to page 12.

60

You must save yourself and Bruce. Your instinct takes over as you reach for a short length of pipe on the floor of the truck and lunge at the larger of the two men. You hit his hand with the pipe. He backs off, howling with pain, and you jump out of the truck. But where is the other man? Wham! He gets you from behind.

You wake up bound hand and foot in a small compartment. You can tell you're aboard an airplane from the sound and the vibrations.

Your uncle is tied up next to you. He has a wide, bloodstained bandage around his head.

"Where are we?" you ask. "And who are these people?"

"I'm not positive. But my suspicion is that we've been kidnapped by the infamous Dr. Ptah."

Turn to page 69.

"I got a note from a man at the airport that said the same thing!" you tell Hassan. "I showed it to Bruce yesterday."

"Is this true?" Hassan asks Bruce.

"I'm afraid it is," Bruce answers. "However, the Sphinx is mute enough at the moment. As soon as the instruments are installed underground, we can start our experiments."

"The electrical lines have not yet been strung in the tunnel," says Hassan, "but I have a flashlight for each of us, and also a strong rope in case we need it. Now we are ready to descend."

Turn to page 40.

When you are finished dressing, the niche widens to become a door. You step into a large chamber. You find that the humming comes from a chorus gathered around a large stone sarcophagus. Inside this is a coffin in the shape of a person. The lid floats a few feet in the air. On one end of the lid is a lifelike sculpture in gold. With a shock you recognize it. It is your own face.

Turn to page 66.

Did Mohammed push you into the well? Did you really slip and fall? You can't tell. You grit your teeth and wonder how far you will fall before you hit bottom. You can still hear the humming. It grows louder. You *should* be terrified—falling down a bottomless shaft in the center of an ancient pyramid, maybe to your death. But you are strangely calm. The musical note seems to have something to do with it. And your rate of falling has slowed. A strong blast of air from below is cushioning your fall.

Suddenly you land—on your feet. You look around you, amazed. You are on a small platform in the center of an amphitheater of some sort. Around you in a circle are nine white-robed figures on large stone thrones. A central figure sitting on the largest throne speaks:

"We have been expecting you."

Turn to page 79.

Against your will you walk up a short flight of stairs. Your mind struggles against it, but the movements of your body are no longer in your control. You lie down in the coffin. The horrible realization of what is happening fills you with panic—but you are now powerless to move.

The lid comes down and covers you. You hear the heavy, grinding sound as the stone lid of the sarcophagus, weighing many tons, slides into place.

There is no way out now. You will lie there as long as the stars rise and set over the desert. You have become part of the secret of the Pyramids.

The End

You are not sure what is going to happen to you in the pyramid, but if Bruce and Andrea want to go in, you don't see how you can refuse.

All three of you enter. The door closes behind you.

"This is a data module," a voice begins. "I will respond telepathically to your brain waves and will answer all of your questions."

"What is the *real* secret of the Pyramids?" you ask.

"This module *is* the secret," the voice answers. "It was left here by the galactic traveler Imhotep in star year four billion ninety-four. This module was connected by hyperspace relay to the main galactic computer located in the Sirius star system. Other pyramids were built to imitate this shape so that the secret could be protected until the right time."

The door to the module reopens, and the three of you step out into the sunlight.

"This is the greatest discovery of my life," Bruce says after a few moments of silence. "This is even more exciting than what I had hoped to find when I came to Egypt. It would be catastrophic if this secret fell into the wrong hands. But if we use its information properly, we might be able to solve all of the problems of the world."

The End

"I can do without your infirmary," says Bruce. "The only thing I want is a ride out of here."

"All in good time, all in good time. First, I must explain to you that I am Ptah, direct descendant of the pharaohs. I am here to complete their work. I intend to conquer the world."

"And just how do you plan to pull off that little feat?" asks Bruce.

"With your help, of course, Professor. Several Russian scientists were on the verge of completing a particle-beam ray gun. By various means I have had them brought here. They have almost completed their work. And now, with you to help them, they will be done in no time at all. When it is finished, the ray will be directed at a mirror on a space platform that I have already placed in orbit around the earth. I will then be able to bounce the ray back to any point on earth, utterly destroying the targets that I choose. If you refuse to help me, you will be imprisoned on the space platform. I give you exactly one hour to make up your mind."

The guards take you and Bruce to a small room with barred windows and lock you in.

If you and Bruce pretend to go along with Ptah in order to play for time, turn to page 11.

If you think that you should try to escape without delay, turn to page 111.

"Dr. Ptah! Who is that?" you ask.

But Bruce has no time to answer. The plane is landing. The door of the small compartment opens. Three men grab you and Bruce by the ankles and pull you out of the plane, dumping you on the ground like two sacks of potatoes.

You look around. You're at one end of a long, narrow, sandy island, bare except for a few palm trees and a large pyramid-shaped building. Down the beach there is a pier with a motor launch moored to it. One of the men cuts the ropes on your feet and wrists, then does the same for Bruce. More men appear, carrying rifles.

"All right," one of them orders, "you two march toward the building over there."

As you walk, you realize just how large the pyramid building is. Though clearly not a solid structure like the ancient pyramids—it has rows of windows at various heights—it is still twenty or thirty stories high. A large mast of some sort rises from the top. The mast is bent sideways to a crazy angle.

An electronically controlled door slides open at the base of the pyramid, and you are pushed inside.

"Take them to the throne room," you hear one of the guards order.

Turn to page 27.

The three of you just make it back into the tunnel when an explosion rocks the room and a section of the floor crashes into some unknown abyss below. Then there is silence. Clouds of dust rise from the gaping hole. You wait for several minutes, hardly daring to breathe.

"I think that's all that is going to happen for the moment," says Hassan.

"Hold on to my legs," says Bruce. He crawls back into the room and leans over the edge of the opening, playing his flashlight down into the space below. "Seems to be some kind of chamber, probably an ancient tomb. The floor is about fifteen feet down. It's lucky we brought a rope along."

"This is a great discovery!" exclaims Hassan. "We must climb down at once."

"I don't know if we should all go," says Bruce, looking at you. "We don't know what kind of a sticky situation we might be getting into. It might be better if you run back and bring help while Hassan and I climb down."

If you convince Bruce that you should share in the discovery of the chamber, turn to page 24.

If you agree to go back for assistance while they investigate, turn to page 90.

"If there are, I've never heard them, or heard of them," Ahmed replies.

You pick out the highest dune nearby and climb it. You reach the top and look down into a huge valley. The sand itself is bright, but in the valley is something even brighter—so dazzling that it blinds you. Ahmed shields his eyes with his hands. "What an incredible sight," he gasps.

Turn to page 55.

You decide you can trust Serena to help you escape.

She slides the iron cot over to the door, wedging it closed. And just in time! You hear loud, angry voices on the other side as someone bangs and struggles to get in. You and Serena jump onto the cot. She cups her hands to give your foot a boost up. Her lift sends you sailing through the window.

Flat rooftops stretch in all directions, lit with a silvery light from the moon. You turn to help Serena climb up, but she is already beside you.

"Quickly, to the other end of the roof," she orders.

You dash across the roof. "They're coming after us!" Serena shouts. "Jump across to the other roof."

You look across and then down. You can't tell how many stories the drop is, but it looks like a long way down. The gap seems terrifyingly wide. Can you make it if you jump?

If you decide to jump, turn to page 103.

If you decide to take a chance with the people who are after you, turn to page 108.

"I've had enough of being cooped up in narrow passageways under umpteen tons of rock," you say.

"Very well," says Mohammed. "Perhaps I can take you on a daytime tour of Cairo."

You agree. After a couple of hours of walking through museums, touring ancient mosques and city walls, and looking at parks and monuments, you are very tired. Mohammed finds a colorful café on one of the broad boulevards in the modern section of Cairo where you can sit and watch the people go by. You have been sitting there for awhile when you notice that Mohammed seems very uneasy.

"Is anything wrong?" you ask.

"Do not move or look around. Several men who I believe are terrorists have surrounded us. How they found us, I do not know. They may have been following us for some time. I can try to get to a phone, or we can make a run for it. Since our chances are about the same either way, I will leave the decision up to you."

If you decide to let Mohammed telephone for help, turn to page 54.

If you decide to make a run for the car, turn to page 30.

You stay on the platform and the walls of the chamber re-form around you. The triangular screen reappears, and the images change and flash before you faster and faster. You see more pyramids being built. Now a different culture takes hold. You recognize the Romans in their military helmets. Christian crosses begin to appear. Churches are built, then swept away in a flash. You recognize the signs of Islam, the mosques with their minarets. Then you get a brief glimpse of Napoleon in his characteristic pose, hand in jacket, before the Pyramids. Then a sign of modern times: an airplane flies over.

The screen fades for a moment. When the images continue, you see tall, strange-looking structures in the distance and flying machines of a design you don't recognize. The screen blurs again. The Pyramids are still there, but the tall structures in the background are gone. The area behind the Pyramids—to the horizon—has been transformed into a green, tree-dotted park. Finally the screen goes blank.

Go to the next page.

The monorail craft silently takes the three of you back to the room where you started. A few minutes later you are making your way toward the surface.

"Remarkable!" says Hassan. "That viewscreen took us back to ancient Egypt and then showed us all of the different periods of Egyptian history since."

"Those last scenes are what amazed me," says Bruce. "Those flying machines we saw haven't even been invented yet, and that beautiful park replacing the desert around the Pyramids . . ."

You are the first to emerge from underground. What you see makes you gasp. Grass and parkland extend in all directions as far as you can see. Overhead are those flying machines of the future.

The End

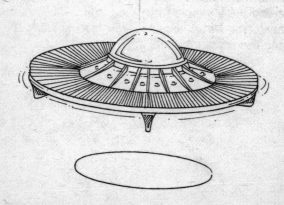

"Maybe it is better for everyone concerned if I wait at your villa," you tell Ahmed.

"All right," he agrees. "I'm certain that you've worked up a real appetite after your adventure. We will eat early tonight."

After dinner you toss and turn for hours. It is difficult for you to sleep, worrying about Bruce. Finally you do fall asleep. When you wake up, it is already late in the morning. Ahmed has long since left to take charge of the raid. You walk around the villa. It is very large, with marble floors, wide hallways, and high ceilings. But there is an ominous silence about the place.

You decide to leave. It might be a good idea to go back to the hotel and look for Andrea.

When you reach the front door, an armed guard stops you. You go back down the long hallway until you find a telephone in one of the rooms. The phone doesn't work. You suddenly realize that you are a prisoner!

Turn to page 20.

"I'm not sure where I am," you say. "Am I still inside the pyramid?"

"This chamber is the lowest point of an inverted pyramid, the exact mirror image of the one above. This is the true magical form discovered by the ancients. Only the upper, aboveground half of this form is known to those outside our order. We are revealing our secret to you because we hope that you will join us. Your uncle is one of our initiates. He is now in great danger. If you become a member of our order, you will be much better equipped to find him."

"What do I have to do to join?" you ask.

"Psychic energy is collected above and then concentrated down here. This energy will transform your being—and initiate you into the Order of Light. However, I must warn you that, if you accept these powers, you will also be given profound responsibilities. Your life can no longer be a simple one, but must be dedicated to fighting the forces of darkness."

If you decide that it might help you to find Bruce if you join, turn to page 28.

If the whole thing sounds too far out to go along with, turn to page 82.

Just before dawn the next morning you and Ahmed leave in his small scout helicopter.

You fly east across the desert. The faintest light begins to creep along the edge of the sky. Then a thin layer of red, like glowing embers, grows along the horizon.

"I plan to mark the route to the terrorists' camp by dropping small smoke bombs in the desert at twenty-mile intervals," Ahmed explains. "The troop-carrying helicopters will leave from a nearby army base in half an hour. They will follow the smoke trail."

As the huge, fiery disc of the sun floats majestically up into the sky, Ahmed notices some dark clouds low on the horizon to the southeast.

Soon strong gusts of wind begin to buffet the helicopter. Ahmed radios the base.

"Come in, ground control. Abort mission for the present. Weather conditions unfavorable."

Ahmed begins a wide bank to the north. The wind is stronger now, and steady. The air is filled with a strange fog. The helicopter begins to cough.

"The dust is beginning to clog the air intake of the engine," says Ahmed. "The air filter can handle normal dust conditions, but we've blundered into a sandstorm."

"Is there anything that we can do?" you ask as the wind begins to howl.

Go on to the next page.

"We have two choices," hollers Ahmed, trying to be heard over the sound of the wind. "We can try to fly through this mess—though I can't believe we'll make it—or we can land and try to find a place to hide from the storm on the ground, but that is unlikely in this part of the desert. We are done for either way. What do *you* think we should do?"

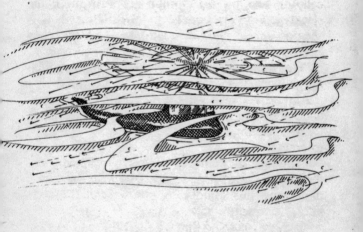

If you think it is better to keep flying,
turn to page 92.

If you think you should land while you have a
chance, turn to page 45.

"I think I'll stay just the way I am," you say. "I'll find Bruce my own way."

"Very well," says the speaker. "Obviously you were not meant to be one of the Chosen."

"You're right," you say. "I don't . . . I don't . . ."

You can't complete the sentence—you feel yourself blacking out.

You awaken outside the pyramid. You are lying on the ground, and Mohammed is putting a damp cloth on your forehead.

"Ow! My head!" you say as you try to sit up. "What happened in the pyramid? I don't remember."

"You hit your head on the low doorway of that last room. You knocked yourself out," says Mohammed. "Do not be embarrassed. Many do it in the dim corridors within the pyramid."

Just then your uncle and Andrea rush up with Ahmed.

Go on to the next page.

"Uncle Bruce!" you exclaim. "Am I glad to see you. I thought you were a goner when they took you off in that truck."

"We caught some of the gang members just as they were trying to smuggle your uncle out of the city," says Ahmed. "We also have reports that a severe sandstorm wiped out the terrorists' headquarters in the desert."

Later, back at the hotel, Bruce tells you some disappointing news.

"For some reason my instruments under the pyramid do not seem to be working properly. I think I'll have to go back to the States and redesign them. When I come back here the next time, do you want to come along again?"

"Now *that* is going to be hard to decide," you answer.

The End

You are anxious to get to the hotel to find Bruce and Andrea. You feel you cannot go to Serena's village.

You thank Serena for her help and slip out of the cart.

Where are you? The pale moon lights up an eerie landscape. Stretching in every direction are small buildings, all deserted. You wander up and down the silent streets until you finally see a group of people huddled in front of a small fire. The night is cool, and they gesture for you to join them. You stay with them until dawn.

With the light of day you realize that you are in a very large cemetery. Those small buildings must be tombs! You're not sure of the way out, but you pick a direction and keep going. Finally you reach a small store just outside the cemetery. You find a telephone and call Bruce at the hotel.

"Bruce," you begin, "I'm in this store just outside of a huge cemetery; where all the tombs are miniature buildings, and . . ."

"I know *exactly* where that is," says Bruce. "Just sit tight until I get there. I'm leaving right away."

In the cab on the way back to the hotel you are almost relieved when Bruce tells you that he has to rush back to the States on urgent business and that you and he are booked on the next flight to New York.

The End

After what seems like hours, the wind begins to die down and the sky lightens a bit. Somehow you and Ahmed have survived. You rub the caked dirt out of your eyes. You massage your legs to get the circulation back. Ahmed produces a small canteen from his belt, and you take a sip. It helps a little. You stand up and look around. There is no trace of the helicopter. Hills and valleys of glistening sand stretch endlessly in all directions.

"We must decide if we should stay here and hope that rescue planes find us or if we should head out across the desert," says Ahmed. "I couldn't tell whether our last message got through or not. If it did, I think we should stay here. If it didn't, I think we should push on. What do you think we should do?"

If you think you should stay where you are, turn to page 101.

If you want to start out across the desert, turn to page 93.

You wake up to find yourself lying on an iron cot in a small storeroom. You sit up and try to move, and find that one ankle is chained to the bed.

Gradually your eyes become accustomed to the darkness. There is a small window high above you on the wall, and through it you can see a crescent moon shining. You can hear the beat of the music you heard in the café. You sit there in the half-darkness trying to figure out how to pick the ancient-looking padlock that secures the chain on your ankle.

The door to the room opens slightly, throwing a shaft of light inside. It's bright enough for you to recognize the dancer from the café. Quietly she closes the door and whispers in your ear.

"My name is Serena. I will help you escape."

She inserts a long, thin bar into the padlock on your ankle. The lock snaps open.

"Here, quickly!" she says. "Stand on my shoulders and climb out the window. It leads to a rooftop. I will pull myself up and follow."

You want to go with her, but you have no idea who this woman is and where she might be leading you. She could be getting you into a worse situation. You look at the window high up on the wall and then at the open door in front of you.

---

*If you decide to accept Serena's help,
turn to page 73.*

*If you don't trust her, and try to escape through
the door, turn to page 104.*

The door to Bruce's room flies open when you yell.

"Let's get out of here fast—and I mean *fast!*" he shouts.

Bruce makes an end run around the snake and out the door to the hallway, pushing you ahead. He slams the door shut.

BLAM! There is a sharp explosion from Bruce's room. People in nightclothes come staggering half-awake out of their rooms.

You meet Andrea in the hallway. She tosses a long native jacket to you. Quickly you throw it on.

"We'll take the back stairway down to the basement," says Bruce. "I have a special car—built for my underwater exploration of the Nile—down there."

When you get there, the three of you jump into the car, and Bruce starts it up. He heads directly for the wall! At the last moment an electronically controlled door opens, and the car shoots into a pool of water on the other side of the door. The car sinks until it is completely underwater, and then it starts forward.

Turn to page 94.

You go back up the shaft, using the hand rope to help pull yourself along. After a short way—it seems *very* soon this time—the shaft levels out. But you walk on and on—and see no exit. You stop and go back. You reach the point where the shaft goes down, but now the hand rope is missing. Where are you? In a panic you run back the other way. Your heart is pounding and your palms are sweaty.

Now you edge carefully forward, pointing your flashlight down seemingly endless passageways. You reach a fork in the tunnel. You don't remember a fork there before! Your hands and knees are shaking, but you force yourself to go on. More forks! You have somehow blundered into a maze of tunnels.

You stop for a moment to think. How can you possibly find your way out? Then you remember a rule to follow when you're trapped in a maze: "Every time you reach a fork, turn right." Remembering this calms your nerves somewhat. Now maybe you have a chance.

Wearily you start to retrace your steps. You just hope that the rule works. At best you know that it will be a long walk.

The End

"It is better to do something—anything—rather than sit here and wait to die," you say.

Ahmed scrapes his digital watch free of dirt. "It's 1:10 P.M. It is already afternoon," he says. "Our best bet is to head west, toward the sun. Later we can follow it as it sets. In the morning we will head away from the rising sun. If the sun becomes obscured by haze, we will stay where we are. Otherwise we will run the risk of wandering around in circles."

You start off. Up and down sand dunes, and then up and down again. Occasionally you stop to wet your lips from Ahmed's canteen.

Then you see it. An oasis shimmers in the distance—a glistening pond surrounded by palm trees.

"Look, look!" you say to Ahmed. Ahmed is strangely calm.

"I'm sorry, but that is just a mirage—a trick the desert plays on the eyes, my friend," he says.

After another mile or so of hiking, you realize that Ahmed is right. Nothing is there. Sheets of water seem to materialize, then vanish after you have walked a few yards.

A few hours later, you stop suddenly. "Ahmed, am I crazy or do I hear thunder in the distance? Are there sound mirages in the desert?"

Turn to page 72.

The submersible car journeys up the river, just under the surface of the water.

"Not long ago," says Bruce, "I discovered the entrance to an underwater tunnel that goes from the Nile to the famous step pyramid at Sakkara. They say Imhotep's tomb is there. I haven't had a chance to explore this tunnel until now."

When you reach Sakkara, the car enters the underwater tunnel. Soon you surface on a broad lake in an underground cavern. In the center of the lake is an island, and in the center of the island is a small pyramid about thirty feet high. It is made of a dull, silvery metal—perhaps platinum. Bruce steers the car to the edge of the island. The three of you jump ashore. As you do, a large opening appears in the side of the pyramid. A voice comes from inside.

"If you wish to know the secret of Imhotep, and the secret of the Pyramids," says the voice, "then *all* of you must step inside."

"I guess it's all or nothing," says Bruce.

Andrea and Bruce want to go in—which leaves it up to you.

*If you decide to go into the pyramid,
turn to page 67.*

*If you feel it might be a trap,
turn to page 109.*

A waiter brings you a long-handled pot containing thick, strong coffee. He pours it ceremoniously into a small porcelain cup. It tastes somewhat bitter, but not too bad. You sip it slowly as you watch the dancing. Is it your imagination, or does the dancer keep glancing in your direction?

The music grows louder. The lights get brighter. You can't seem to focus your eyes. Your arms and legs feel like lead, and you can't move them. You feel dizzy. You feel like you are passing out!

Turn to page 87.

"OK," says Bruce, "let's all three give it a shot."

You feel a lot better going along than waiting alone in that spooky room.

As soon as you are on board, Bruce pushes one of the buttons on the control panel. There is a whirring sound and the door of the strange craft slides shut with an ominous click.

The bubble starts smoothly along the rail and into the tunnel. After a minute or so, it slows to a stop. The bubble door opens and the three of you climb out. You find yourselves in a chamber almost identical to the one you just left. However, this room seems to have no exit. This does not seem logical to you. Whoever created this transportation system would hardly have built it just for the ride.

On a hunch, you feel carefully along the wall. Jackpot! Two triangular panels recess into the wall and slide apart, revealing a large room with slanted walls.

"Good work," says Bruce.

The three of you enter. As you look around you realize that you are in a room shaped like the *inside* of a pyramid.

Suddenly the triangular door closes behind you and disappears. You are trapped inside! The walls—four perfect triangles—begin to glow brighter and brighter.

Turn to page 18.

Up ahead you see another oasis. Is it another mirage? You head for it anyway. One part of the desert is as good as any other when it comes to leaving your sun-dried bones.

You get there first. "This *is* water! Actual water!" you exclaim. "This is not a mirage!"

You dunk your entire head in the water. Nothing has ever felt better in your life.

Later, when you are both rested, Ahmed says, "Some of these palm trees are date palms with fruit. We will have enough food and water until the next caravan arrives. It is only a matter of time before we are rescued."

The End

You repeat Al-Din's spell three times. The room begins to spin around you, then fades away altogether. You seem to be floating in a void. Are you asleep? Dreaming? You find yourself flying high up over the ocean on what could be a magic carpet.

You awaken in your living room back home. The phone is ringing. You answer it. Your uncle is on the phone.

"I'm just in from Egypt," he says. "I have to get some new equipment to continue my investigations of the Pyramids. How would you like to go back with me for a few weeks?"

This is really strange. Did you just dream everything that happened, or did that magician really send you back here to start over?

If you decide that it was just a dream, and you would still like to go, turn to page 2.

If you say no, knowing what is in store for you, turn to page 113.

"I'm sure the radio message got through," you say.

"I think so too," says Ahmed. "The best thing to do is to wait where we are."

Ahmed digs around in the sand where you crouched during the storm.

"Here they are," says Ahmed, "the smoke bombs. I was afraid that I had lost them. Each one of these will send out smoke for an hour."

Ahmed sets off one of the bombs. A tall column of smoke rises in the now still air.

The last one is set off late in the afternoon. "This is it," says Ahmed. "If no one sees *this* smoke, we may be out of luck."

Just as the smoke begins to disappear, you hear the drone of a plane. It banks and makes a low pass over you.

"They see us!" you shout, jumping up and down on the sand.

The plane, which belongs to the Egyptian Air Force, lands nearby. You are saved this time. You wonder how many adventures lie ahead before you get back to the States.

The End

Turn to page 117.

You might as well take a chance and try the jump. You step back a few feet, make a short run, and take a flying leap to the other roof. You manage to grab the edge with your hands as you slip down along the side of the building. You struggle to pull yourself up. You are about to lose your grip when a strong arm grabs you by the wrist and heaves you onto the roof. It's Serena!

"Wow!" you exclaim. "Are all belly dancers as strong as you are?"

"I was trained to be an acrobat by my family," she says, "before I was kidnapped by the evil gang that owns the café."

"Why haven't you tried to escape before?" you ask.

"I have," she says, "but it's not that easy. They control this quarter of Cairo completely. Now my family has discovered where I am and has arranged my escape—but you will see. We must hurry. I hear someone coming."

Turn to page 110.

You pull open the door and dash down a corridor that leads back into the café. You run outside. Two men from the café race after you, shouting in Arabic. You push your way through the crowds, trying to stay hidden. Which way to go? There is an open door on your right with a small courtyard inside. You decide to chance it and dart through the door, slamming it behind you. You lean against the door, gasping for breath.

A hulk of a man appears. He has a heavy, dark beard and piercing eyes.

"Welcome to my house," he says. "Have you come to buy a magic spell or perhaps something to ward off the evil eye?"

"I need help," you say. "Someone is after me."

"In that case, you are welcome in my humble house. You are safe here. I am Al-Din, the magician. My magic will protect you."

You follow Al-Din up a flight of stairs into a room with a low table surrounded by cushions. He serves you some mint tea and tells you about the ancient magic he practices.

"All is illusion," he says. "Here, I will show you. Close your eyes and repeat this spell three times: *abah arah arah abah blah ah.*"

Turn to page 100.

"Hurry inside," Andrea says, "and close the door behind you."

The room you enter is dark, and it takes a few moments for your eyes to adjust to the light. When they do, you see Andrea in front of you with a revolver in her hand, silencer and all. The gun is pointed at you.

"Kill! I must kill. . . ." she says in a mechanical-sounding voice. Her eyes are glassy, as if she were hypnotized.

"Andrea, what are you saying?" you gasp.

"The secrets must be protected . . . must be protected. . . ." she continues in that same strange voice. It sounds almost like a recording.

You realize with a shudder that Andrea's mind has been taken over by some evil force.

"Andrea!" you shout. "I don't *know* any secrets. I don't even know what's going on. Someone has done something to you. You don't know what you are doing."

She raises the gun to fire.

"Andrea! No!" you cry.

But the *pffut* of the silencer ends it for you.

The End

The gap to the next roof is just too wide. You know that you would never make it across. Serena, however, is already across and has disappeared.

You turn to face your pursuers. Then you recognize them.

"Bruce! Andrea!" you exclaim. "It's you. How did you get here?"

"The cab driver who brought you here was worried," Bruce says. "He went to the police and they called us."

Suddenly you realize that you've got to stop Serena from running away. The three of you can help her.

"Serena, come back!" you shout. "These are my friends."

The sound of your voice echoes across the rooftops, but there is no reply.

You, Bruce, and Andrea return to the hotel. Your parents are on the overseas phone. They have begun to worry about you and insist that you return home.

Back in the States you find that many of your friends do not believe your story, especially the part about your new friend the belly dancer.

The End

"You have thirty seconds left," says the voice from inside the pyramid. "After that, you may no longer enter."

"I'm not just going to walk into that thing," you say. "Not unless I know more about it."

"If that's your honest choice," says Bruce, "Andrea and I will respect it. And in that case, I guess we'll all stay out."

"This module will now suspend operations for one galactic minute—which is four hundred and seventy-five Earth years," says the voice.

The door closes. You can find no trace of it on the surface of the pyramid.

"I wonder what would have happened if we *had* gone inside?" you ask.

"Well, we can come back in four hundred and seventy-five years and find out," says Bruce.

"Or we can come back now with special equipment," says Andrea, "and try to pry its secrets loose."

You are already looking forward to *that*.

The End

Serena leads you down a long flight of stairs.

You follow her through passageways that are so narrow you can barely squeeze through. Sometimes you can hear shouting nearby and see the flickering beams of flashlights searching the dark corners where you were standing only seconds before. Finally, in a narrow alley, Serena stops and listens for a few moments.

"See that donkey cart over there," she whispers. "It is from my village. I have arranged for it to meet me here. I will crawl into the bottom of it. Watch how I do it, then follow."

There is just room enough for you to squeeze into the cart. Serena arranges the straw over the two of you and then signals to the driver with a low whistle.

The cart starts off. You go through narrow alleyways, then down larger streets. Gradually the street noises die away, and you guess that you are outside the city.

"I think we are safely away from our pursuers," says Serena. "If you wish, you may find your way from here. If you continue with me to my village, you will be welcome there."

*If you decide to get out of the cart,
turn to page 84.*

*If you decide to continue on to Serena's village,
turn to page 114.*

"Even if we seem to be cooperating," you say, "Ptah will finish us off as soon as we stop being useful to him."

"I think you're right," says Bruce. "When the guards come for us, we'll jump them. I don't think they expect us to fight back. It might take them by surprise."

"At least we won't be giving up without a struggle," you say.

The guards *are* taken by surprise. The fight is brief and furious, but there are just too many of them. The guards overpower you and drag you back to Ptah.

"Take them to the other end of the island," he shouts.

Go on to the next page.

Again you are tied up and carried off. You are taken to the other end of the island where a rocket is ready to blast off to resupply Ptah's orbiting space station. You and Bruce are dumped into a small compartment in the rocket.

You are already working your hands free as you blast off.

"The crew is going to be too busy for awhile to bother about us," you say. "If we can break out of this compartment and get the jump on them, maybe we can take over the ship. Then we can put Ptah's space station out of action for good."

You know that you'll need a lot of luck to get out of *this* situation—a lot more than you're likely to get.

The End

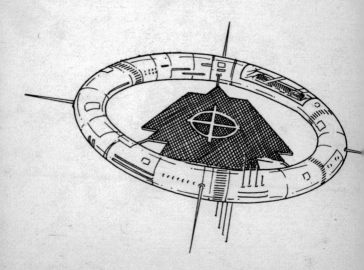

"I'd really like to go," you say, "but I have a lot of work at school, and I already have tickets for a play at the end of the month. Thanks for asking— and have a good trip."

Your excuses sound a bit thin, but you've just gone through a harrowing experience. Even if you only dreamed it, you're not going through *that* again!

The End

You don't really know where you are. It might be safer to go all the way to Serena's village.

You ride for another few hours. There is utter silence except for the clip-clop of the donkey's hooves and the creak of the wheels. You drift off to sleep. Sometime later Serena shakes you gently.

"We are here, at my village, and with my people."

You crawl out of the cart. Dawn is just breaking. You are near a field. In the center you see a large bonfire. Around the fire are hundreds of figures in white turbans and white robes. They are chanting in unison—it's an eerie sound. Then the figures rise and begin to move together around the fire in a strange, slow dance, rolling their heads and chanting, *"Allah-Allah-ah-ah."* The hypnotic effect of the dancing draws you in, and you join the circle.

Turn to page 116.

You stay with Serena's people, one of the many tribes of Dervishes, for several days while she manages to get word secretly to Bruce that you are safe.

At last Bruce and Andrea arrive at the village.

"Thank goodness you're all right," says Bruce. "Andrea and I followed your trail to the café. The police raided the place and uncovered a nest of foreign agents code named SPHINX. But by then you were gone. Later, when we returned to the hotel, we found Serena's note telling us where you were.

"Unfortunately, I had to tell your parents that you were missing. They have been very worried. I guess you'd better catch a plane home and show them that you are really all right. I am sorry you had only one day in Egypt."

Back in the States, whenever you see the dawn, you think of those white-robed figures chanting their hymn to the first light of day.

You weren't in Egypt very long, but it was an adventure you'll never forget.

The End

DO YOU LOVE CHOOSE YOUR OWN ADVENTURE®?

Let your younger brothers and sisters in on the fun.

You know how great CHOOSE YOUR OWN ADVENTURE® books are to read and reread. But did you know that there are CHOOSE YOUR OWN ADVENTURE® books for younger kids too? They're just as thrilling as the CHOOSE YOUR OWN ADVENTURE® books you read and they're filled with the same kinds of decisions and different ways for the stories to end—but they're shorter with more illustrations and come in a larger, easier-to-read size.

So get your younger brothers and sisters and anyone else you know between the ages of seven and nine in on the fun by introducing them to the exciting world of CHOOSE YOUR OWN ADVENTURE®.

Bantam CHOOSE YOUR OWN ADVENTURE® books for younger readers, on sale wherever paperbacks are sold:

#1 THE CIRCUS by Edward Packard
#2 THE HAUNTED HOUSE by R. A. Montgomery
#3 SUNKEN TREASURE by Edward Packard
#4 YOUR VERY OWN ROBOT by R. A. Montgomery
#5 GORGA, THE SPACE MONSTER by Edward Packard
#6 THE GREEN SLIME by R. A. Montgomery
#7 HELP! YOU'RE SHRINKING by Edward Packard
#8 INDIAN TRAIL by R. A. Montgomery

AV7—4/83

ABOUT THE AUTHOR

RICHARD BRIGHTFIELD is a graduate of Johns Hopkins University, where he studied biology, psychology, and archaeology. He worked for many years as a graphic designer at Columbia University. In addition, he has coauthored more than a dozen game books with his wife, Glory. The Brightfields and their daughter, Savitri, live in Gardiner, New York.

ABOUT THE ILLUSTRATOR

ANTHONY KRAMER graduated from the Paier School of Art in Hamden, Connecticut, where he received the Children's Book Illustration award. He has been an editorial cartoonist, an architectural artist, and a designer of children's toy packages. He has illustrated eight books for children, including *Underground Kingdom* by Edward Packard for Bantam's Choose Your Own Adventure® series. Mr. Kramer lives in New York City where he loves to walk, run, and bicycle.